THE MONKEY KING
Converts to Buddhism

Based on *Journey to the West*
by Wu Cheng'en

WFP
WordFire Press

朝華出版社
BLOSSOM PRESS

New Translation by Li Chaoyuan
Illustrations by Zeng Zhao'an & Liu Jikun

EBook ISBN: 978-1-68057-482-1
Trade Paperback ISBN: 978-1-68057-483-8
Hardcover ISBN: 978-1-68057-484-5

Cover design by Janet McDonald
Adapted by Firethorn
Review by Scott Huntsman
Edited and Adapted by Rebecca Moesta
Published by
WordFire Press, LLC
PO Box 1840
Monument CO 80132

Kevin J. Anderson & Rebecca Moesta, Publishers
WordFire Press eBook Edition 2022
WordFire Press Trade Paperback Edition 2022
WordFire Press Hardcover Edition 2022
Printed in the USA

Join our WordFire Press Readers Group for
sneak previews, updates, new projects, and giveaways.

Sign up at wordfirepress.com

Review

Previously, the Monkey King (Sun Wukong), visited the Dragon King of the Eastern Ocean and took a magic Gold-Banded Staff to serve as his weapon. This caused an earthquake, and the Dragon King filed a complaint with Heaven.

The Jade Emperor invited the Monkey King to Heaven and appointed him Heavenly Stable Supervisor. The menial position angered Wukong, so he returned to his tribe and proclaimed himself the Great Sage Equal to Heaven.

To appease Monkey, the Jade Emperor let him keep the title Great Sage Equal to Heaven and made him Supervisor of the Immortal-Peach Orchard. Later, Wukong learned he wasn't invited to the Grand Peach Feast. He was so insulted that he wrecked the banquet and went home again.

The Jade Emperor sent heavenly soldiers down to capture Wukong, but they could not defeat him. After a long, hard battle, they finally captured Monkey and threw him into an alchemy furnace to burn.

The Monkey King wasn't hurt, though, and he gained the power of all-seeing fiery eyes. Wukong kicked his way out of the furnace and wreaked havoc in the Jade Emperor's throne room.

After being captured by Heaven for making a disturbance, Wukong spent forty-nine days in the Taoist Master's furnace. The Great Sage was not only unharmed, but the alchemical fire refined his eyes gave him all-seeing vision. When he jumped out of the furnace and created havoc in the Jade Emperor's throne room, no one could stop him. So the Jade Emperor sent a holy messenger to the Western Continent to ask Buddha Tathagata for help subduing Monkey.

The messenger arrived at Buddha Tathagata's temple and explained the situation.

"Please stay here and perform your duties as usual," the Buddha told his Bodhisattvas. "I will be away helping the Jade Emperor." He then headed for Heaven with two of his primary disciples, Ananda and Kasyapa.

When Buddha Tathagata arrived at the Jade Emperor's throne room, he came face to face with the Monkey King, who had changed himself into a warrior with three heads and six arms. Wielding his gold-banded iron staff, Wukong was in the middle of a fierce fight with thirty-six heavenly generals.

The Buddha ordered the generals to stop fighting and to retreat.

The Monkey King changed back to his true appearance and shouted, "Who are you that you dare to stop my fight?"

"I am the venerable Sakyamuni, Buddha from the Land of Ultimate Bliss on the Western Continent," Buddha Tathagata answered with a smile. "I hear that you are quite unruly—that you run rampant and wild through the countryside and create havoc in Heaven. I wonder … can you tell me why you are so violent?"

"The mortal world feels too confining, and I want to live in Heaven in the Jade Emperor's Hall of Divine Mists," Wukong replied. "If the Jade Emperor agrees, everything will be fine. Otherwise, I will keep raising havoc, and the Heavenly Palace will never be peaceful again."

The Buddha scoffed. "How much power do you have that you think you can just take the celestial throne?"

"I have many abilities," said the Great Sage. "I can do seventy-two transformations and travel by cloud-somersaults, each taking me 108,000 miles. So who can stop me from staying here?"

"Let's make a bet then," suggested the Buddha. "If you can somersault out of my hand, I'll make sure the Jade Emperor approves your request. Deal?"

Wukong laughed, thinking, *The Buddha is an idiot. A single somersault takes me 108,000 miles. Of course I can get out of his hand.* So he agreed and leaped into the Buddha's hand.

Monkey put his iron staff back into his ear and shouted, "Off I go!" He launched a cloud-somersault and soon disappeared.

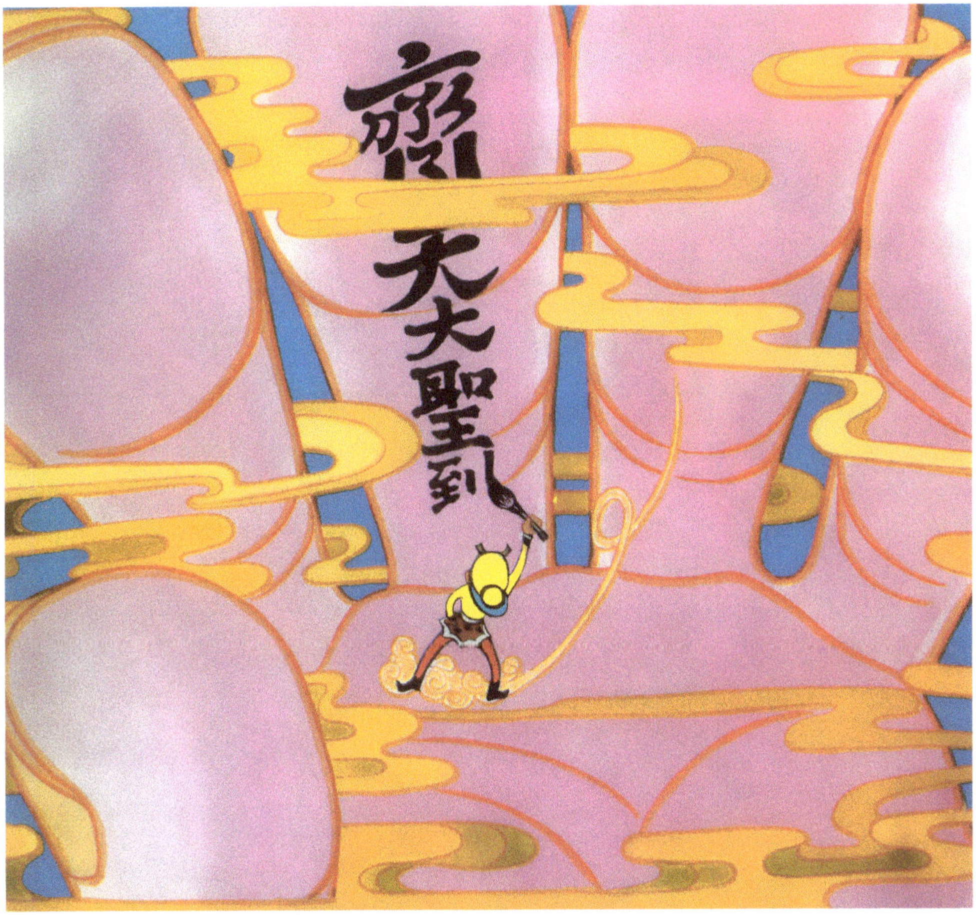

Wukong flew for quite some distance before seeing five pinkish pillars surrounded by mysterious light blue mists. *I must have reached the border of Heaven*, he thought. *I should leave a mark to show that I came this far.* He pulled out a hair, turned it into an ink brush, and wrote on one of the pillars, "The Great Sage Equal to Heaven was here."

Then the Monkey King launched a cloud-somersault to return. When he got back to the Buddha Tathagata's hand, he beamed. "See? I already traveled to the border of Heaven and back. Now hold up your end of the deal."

"You never even made it out of my hand, naughty Monkey," said the Buddha.

"Oh? Come take a look at the mark I left!" Wukong protested.

"There is no need to leave. See the evidence for yourself."

Wukong looked carefully with his all-seeing fiery eyes and found the line of characters written on the Buddha's finger. "The Great Sage Equal to Heaven was here," it said. And the ink was still wet.

I was sure I wrote those words on a pillar holding up the sky, Wukong thought in disbelief. *How did it end up on his finger? I will go and double-check.*

As the Monkey King turned to rush out, the Buddha flipped his hand over and transformed his fingers into a range of five mountain peaks—representing metal, wood, water, fire, and earth—and named it the Mountain of Five Elements.

Wukong was imprisoned under the mountain.

Seeing that Buddha Tathagata had subdued the Great Sage, the Jade Emperor could not have been happier. To celebrate the victory, he invited all deities to a Peace in Heaven Banquet. The immortals sang and danced and ate and drank until a heavenly patrol arrived with bad news. "Monkey is sticking his head out."

"Do not worry, do not worry," said the Buddha. From his sleeve he took out a scroll inscribed with golden writing. He handed it to his disciple Ananda, who went to the Mountain of Five Elements and fixed the scroll tightly to a square rock.

The inscription immediately caused the mountain to sprout roots that wove together, closing all the cracks and seams between rocks. The Monkey King only had room to breathe and to stretch a bit, but he could not escape.

Buddha Tathagata bade the Jade Emperor and the deities farewell. On his way back to the Western Continent, he passed the Mountain of Five Elements and felt compassion. He summoned the guardian deities of the land and of the five directions and asked them to feed the Monkey King iron pellets when he was hungry and give him melted copper when he was thirsty.

And so the Great Sage remained under the mountain. Time flew like an arrow, and more than 500 years passed in the blink of an eye. In the mortal world, Emperor Taizong reigned (627–649 AD) in the Tang Dynasty. One day, Emperor Taizong issued a decree for his ministers to choose a highly regarded Buddhist monk to preach the Buddhist teachings. After an extensive search, his ministers chose Master Xuanzang, who had become a monk at a young age and was greatly respected for his ethics and profound knowledge.

Master Xuanzang gathered 1,200 esteemed Buddhist monks to preach and discuss Buddhist teachings at a temple in the capital of the Tang Dynasty. The Emperor also came to listen to them when he had time.

Emperor Taizong learned that in the East, teachers only taught the early conservative Buddhism called Hinayana. But on the Western Continent where the Buddha lived, they also taught Mahayana Buddhism, which could relieve human pain and suffering.

Emperor Taizong asked the monks, "Who will accept my command and go to the Western Continent to bring back the Mahayana Buddhist scriptures?"

Before the Emperor finished speaking, Master Xuanzang stood up and said, "I am willing, Your Majesty."

Emperor Taizong was pleased and swore brotherhood with Xuanzang. He also gave the monk two precious gifts from Bodhisattva Guanyin: a brocade monk's robe and a nine-ringed pewter staff. The grateful Xuanzang vowed, "Your Majesty, I will spare no effort and dedicate my life to bringing back the scriptures."

The next day, Emperor Taizong personally led his ministers outside the city wall to see the monk off. He gave Xuanzang a purple and gold alms bowl, a horse, and two experienced travelers to accompany him. Xuanzang thanked Emperor Taizong, bade the ministers farewell, and embarked on his journey to the Western Continent.

Xuanzang and the two guides pushed themselves to travel as fast as they could. One day, they set off again at 3:00 in the morning. The frost was clear and the moon was bright, so the road was easy to follow, and they walked for dozens of miles until they reached a mountain. The road became rugged, and they could only find their path by pulling up the tall grass.

As they kept walking, the men worried that they might have gone the wrong way. All of a sudden, they stepped out onto nothing but air. The three men and their horse fell into a pit. Then to their horror, a billowing wind carried fifty to sixty imps straight toward them.

"Seize them! Seize them!" shouted the imps.

The imps captured the men and took them to a cave to meet their monstrous king. The king and a pair of his brawny visitors killed Xuanzang's two assistants. Xuanzang was so frightened he passed out.

When the red sun was high, Xuanzang woke in a daze. An old man stood over him, and with a wave of his hands, he broke the ropes that bound Xuanzang.

"This is Double-Fork Ridge," the old man said. "That monster king you met was a tiger demon, and his murderous friends were a black bear demon and a wild ox demon. Get up and follow me. I will guide you back to your road."

The grateful Xuanzang led his horse out of the pit and followed the old man to the main road. As he was about to thank him, the old man rose on the breeze, mounted a red-crowned crane, and flew into the sky.

A piece of paper drifted down to Xuanzang. It said, "I am the Evening Star, sent to rescue you. On your way, you will meet divine disciples to help you. Do not complain about any hardships on your pilgrimage." Xuanzang bowed toward the sky in gratitude.

Xuanzang walked onward feeling lonely with only his horse for company. He traveled a long time on the mountain without seeing a single person or even a cottage. Suddenly, with a roar, a golden leopard jumped out and sprang at him. Xuanzang's horse fell to the ground in fright and would not get back up.

As hope seemed lost, a brave man with a forked spear leaped down the hillside and faced the leopard. Man and beast fought for nearly an hour. The leopard eventually tired, and the man managed to stab it, pinning the creature to the ground.

The man then helped the frightened Xuanzang get back to his feet and comforted him. "Do not be afraid," he said. "I am a hunter on the mountain. What brought you here?"

"I am a monk sent by the Tang emperor on a pilgrimage to the West to worship the Buddha and ask for scriptures," Xuanzang said. "Thank you so much for saving my life."

"If you were sent by the Tang emperor," said the hunter, "then we are fellow country-men. This mountain is also Tang territory. You are welcome to stay in my house tonight, and I will help you on your way tomorrow." Full of joy, Xuanzang thanked the hunter and followed him to his house, leading the horse.

The next day, the hunter accompanied Xuanzang down the mountain. After walking for half a day, they approached another mountain, tall and steep. As Xuanzang was saying goodbye to the hunter, they heard a thunderous shout at the foot of the mountain.

"My Master is here! My Master is here!" The two men were startled.

"It must be the immortal Monkey shouting," said the hunter. "Several centuries ago, that mountain fell from the sky and imprisoned a divine monkey under it. Come, let me show you." Xuanzang followed him, and they did indeed find a trapped Monkey, sticking out his hands and saying, "Master, what took you so long? I am so happy you are finally here. Please rescue me, and I will protect you on your journey to the Western Continent."

"Which one of us are you talking to?" asked the hunter.

"The Master, of course," the Monkey King said. "I am the Great Sage Equal to Heaven who wreaked havoc in Heaven 500 years ago, so the Buddha imprisoned me here. Bodhisattva Guanyin passed by here once and told me to expect a monk from the Eastern Continent who could set me free. I want to become a Buddhist. I will be your disciple and protect you while you search for the scriptures."

"I can see you have good intentions after being enlightened by Guanyin," replied Xuanzang with delight. "But how can I free you when I have no tools?"

"On top of this mountain on a stone post is a scroll inscribed in gold by the Buddha," the Monkey King said. "All you need to do is climb up there and remove the scroll."

Xuanzang and the hunter climbed the mountain and found the scroll on a slab of rock that shone with golden rays of light. Xuanzang knelt and bowed in respect before taking the gold scroll.

When the pair arrived back at the foot of the mountain, Xuanzang said to Monkey, "I removed the scroll. You can come out now."

Overjoyed, Wukong said, "Thank you, Master! Now please go away so that I can come out and not frighten you."

The hunter led Xuanzang five or seven miles away.

"Go further!" the Monkey King shouted. "Even further!"

The men walked all the way down the mountain. Then, with a loud boom, the ground cracked, the mountain collapsed, and the Great Sage Equal to Heaven appeared next to them.

The Monkey King went to meet Xuanzang officially and bowed four times.

"Dear apprentice, let me give you a disciple name that I will call you by," said Xuanzang.

"Thank you, Master," replied Monkey. "I actually have a disciple name: Sun Wukong."

Xuanzang was delighted. "Very fitting! Then I will give you a nickname. What about Xingzhe—pilgrim monk?" Wukong accepted gladly.

Wukong—now Xingzhe Sun—went to pack up.

"Congratulations on taking a great disciple!" said the hunter to Xuanzang. "I will take my leave now and go home."

Xuanzang thanked him and they parted ways.

After helping Xuanzang mount his horse, Monkey picked up the bags, put them on his back, and walked in front to guide the way.

When they had passed the mountains, a tiger suddenly jumped out, roaring and switching his tail. Xuanzang was terrified.

Pilgrim comforted him. "Do not be afraid, Master. I am here to protect you."

The Monkey King put down the luggage, retrieved the iron needle from his ear, and enlarged it to a massive fighting staff. He held it up, shook it against the wind, and laughed. "It has been five centuries since I last used this little treasure." He stepped forward to meet the tiger head-on.

Sensing the power of the Monkey King, the tiger crouched and stayed still. With one blow of his iron staff, Pilgrim hit its head, and the tiger died.

Xuanzang was astonished. "Oh my goodness! It took many hours for our strong hunter to defeat the golden leopard, but this Monkey killed a tiger without a fight. How powerful he is! The saying is true: For every strong person, there is someone stronger."

Wukong then shrank his weapon to the size of a needle and tucked it back into his ear. He urged Xuanzang to get back on the horse, picked up their luggage, and led the way.

The two moved on. Hours later, they heard a whistle from the roadside, and six bandits stepped into the road carrying spears and bows and short swords. "Hey monks! Leave your horse and bags, and we may spare your life!"

Xuanzang panicked.

"Do not worry, Master," said Pilgrim. "They are here to give us some travel money."

Wukong stepped right up to them. "Hey, petty thieves! Share your stolen treasure with us, and I may spare your lives."

Furious, the bandits attacked in a swarm, slashing seventy or eighty times.

As if bored, Pilgrim stood with his arms folded across his chest as they hacked at him.

Surprised to find Monkey unfazed by earthly weapons, the bandits fled.

Wukong laughed and called after them. "You may be tired of fighting, but now it is my turn to do some needlework." He took out his needle, turned it into a staff, caught up with the thieves, and killed them one by one.

Pilgrim gathered their belongings and returned to Xuanzang with a smile. "Master, I have killed the bandits, so you are safe. Please get on your horse."

Xuanzang gave a sigh of grief and disappointment. "Most Buddhists are so kind that they would not hurt so much as an ant. How could you be so merciless? You killed six people without compassion! Have you already forgotten how your violence put you in prison for five-centuries? You are supposedly a Buddhist, but if you continue this behavior, you will not be able to complete your pilgrimage and become a Buddhist monk."

Wukong had never been able to bear being reprimanded. Annoyed by Xuanzang's teaching, he muttered, "Well, if you say I cannot make it to the Western Continent or become a true Buddhist monk, I may as well go back."

Without waiting for Xuanzang to answer, Monkey flew away eastward with a cloud-somersault.

Xuanzang was left alone and had to march forward by himself. Before long, he saw an old lady coming toward him.

The old lady chatted with Xuanzang. When she learned he was from the Eastern Tang Dynasty on a pilgrimage to the West to study scriptures, she seemed concerned. "What a long way you have to go! How can you make the journey by yourself?"

"I actually took in a disciple recently, but he was quite unruly," Xuanzang answered. "When I scolded him a bit, he abandoned me and headed east in a fit of anger."

"My home is also in the east," said the old lady. "I have a nice cap inlaid with golden flowers. Please take it. I will also teach you a spell to tighten the band inside the hat. You should learn it by heart. I will go catch up with your disciple and persuade him to follow you wholeheartedly. When he returns, give him this hat. If he does not behave, just recite the spell."

Xuanzang bowed his head to thank the old lady. When he looked up, he saw her sit on a lotus throne and rise into the sky as she revealed her true appearance. It had been Bodhisattva Guanyin in disguise! Xuanzang gazed into the sky, praying.

After he left Xuanzang, Wukong took a cloud-somersault directly to Water-Crystal Palace to see the Dragon King of the Eastern Ocean.

The Dragon King greeted him. "Great Sage, I heard that you were recently freed from imprisonment and are now guarding a Tang monk on his pilgrimage. What brings you back here?"

The Monkey King waved his hand. "Forget about him. That ungrateful monk does not know good from bad. I killed several bandits to keep him safe, yet he told me I was wrong to kill them. How could I tolerate such a rebuke? So I came to visit on my way back to my tribe."

"Great Sage, if you do not guard the Tang monk, work hard, and accept teaching, you will never fulfill your potential as a true Buddhist. You have such promise, do not delay your future and idle away your time on the easy life."

Wukong recognized the sense in these words, so he bade the Dragon King farewell, mounted a cloud, and headed back to Xuanzang.

On the way he met Bodhisattva Guanyin in the clouds. "Wukong, why are you not with your Master, the Tang monk, learning from him and protecting him?" she asked. "What are you doing here?"

From his cloud the Monkey King bowed and replied, "When I fought to keep him safe, he judged me violent and unruly. I hid and spent some time alone, but now I am on my way back to him."

Soon, Wukong saw Xuanzang sitting by the road. He descended from the cloud and approached him. "Master, how are you? Why are you here?"

"Pilgrim, I am hungry," Xuanzang replied. "Bring me some bread from my bag."

Opening the bag, the Monkey King saw the gold-inlaid cap.

Wukong admired it and said, "Good Master, may I have this cap?"

Xuanzang nodded.

The Monkey King happily put it on and threw away his old cap.

As soon as Xuanzang saw Pilgrim wearing the cap, he recited the spell.

Monkey felt such terrible pain in his head that he rolled on the ground, yelling, "My head! It hurts! It hurts!" Wukong tried to tear the cap off, but the gold thread formed a band that drew tighter and tighter around his head. The cap would not move, as if it had taken root.

Seeing Pilgrim's pain, Xuanzang stopped reciting the tightening spell.

Pilgrim's head stopped hurting and he realized what had happened. "Master, you caused my headache."

"Who taught you that trick?" Wukong asked.

"An old lady I just met," said Xuanzang.

Wukong was angry. "Say no more. That old lady must have been Guanyin!" He took out his iron staff, ready to fight Xuanzang.

Xuanzang recited the tightening spell again.

Monkey's head began to hurt so badly that he could no longer stand up straight or hold his weapon. "Master, please, stop," he begged. "Please! I'll listen to you."

"Will you still be unruly?" Xuanzang asked sternly.

"No. I would not dare." From then on, Pilgrim was a devoted, obedient, and loyal guard to Xuanzang.

Several days later, the two reached a powerful mountain stream. They heard a huge roar as a dragon lunged up out of the water, jumped onto the bank, and charged straight toward Master Xuanzang. In shock, Wukong dropped the luggage, grabbed his master off the horse, and fled. Pilgrim ran so fast that the dragon was unable to catch them, so it devoured their horse and plunged back into the water.

After settling his master in a safe place, Wukong returned to the stream and found only their luggage. He jumped into the air and looked around with his all-seeing fiery eyes. There was no trace of the horse. Assuming it had been eaten by the dragon, the Monkey King stood on the bank of the stream and shouted, "You barbarous lizard, bring back the horse! Give me back my horse!"

The dragon who had eaten Master Xuanzang's horse was resting at the bottom of the stream nourishing his spirit. When he heard someone yelling at him, however, he launched himself to the surface to confront him. "Who dares to abuse me here?"

"Bring the horse back to me!" shouted Wukong, raising his gold-banded iron staff.

The two opponents fought up and down and back and forth and round and round. They fought for so long that the dragon became weak and tired. At last he turned around, dove back into the stream, swam to the bottom, and refused to come out, making himself deaf to Wukong's tirade.

Pilgrim was almost at his wits' end when he heard someone calling him from the sky. It was Guanyin.

Wukong jumped high into the sky to tell her his grievances. "Good Bodhisattva, why would you want to cause me pain?" he asked. "Why did you make me suffer by teaching my Master that band-tightening spell?"

"Because, dear Monkey, without a method of discipline, you do not follow the teachings or restrain yourself," said Guanyin. "If you made trouble as you did before, who would take care of it? Do not complain and expect me to pay you back."

From above, Bodhisattva Guanyin called out, "Third Prince of the Western Ocean Dragon King, come meet Guanyin, the Bodhisattva of the South Seas!"

The small dragon emerged from the water, became a human, jumped into the sky, and paid homage to Guanyin.

"You were sentenced to death for setting fire to the palace and burning a bright pearl," said Guanyin. "I begged the Jade Emperor to spare your life so you could make amends by assisting the Tang monk in his travels. How is it that you ate his horse instead?" She introduced Wukong. "This is Pilgrim, the monk's first disciple."

"I am sorry," said the dragon. "It was a misunderstanding. They made no mention of scriptures or the Tang."

"Oh Monkey, you are so arrogant that you never think to give other people credit," said Guanyin. "If you go forward, there are more disciples waiting to be converted. In the future, if anyone asks you, mention the scriptures and your pilgrimage first. It will save you a great deal of trouble."

Pilgrim gladly accepted her advice.

Guanyin dipped her willow branch into dew and sprinkled it over the small dragon's body. Then she blew out a magical breath and said, "Change!"

The dragon immediately became a white dragon horse.

"You must work with all your heart to atone for the wrong you have done and fulfill your pilgrimage," instructed Guanyin. "When you succeed, you will no longer be an ordinary dragon. You will receive a golden body."

The dragon horse nodded.

Pilgrim led the dragon horse to meet Xuanzang and told him the whole story. Master Xuanzang was happy with his new steed and bowed to the sky in gratitude to Bodhisattva Guanyin. Then he got up and made ready to travel again.

Pilgrim helped Xuanzang mount the dragon horse and picked up their luggage. Together, they marched on toward the west.

PUBLISHER'S NOTE

All books in our The Irrepressible Monkey King series are based on the Chinese novel *Journey to the West*. Written in the 1500s during the Ming Dynasty by Wu Cheng'en, *Journey to the West* is one of the Four Great Classical Novels of Chinese literature. The story mixes myths and folklore with historical events from the 7th century. There are a few well-known translations into English, some of which are condensed, while others are complete. This book is a new translation into English from an abridged Chinese-language version of *Journey to the West*.

The original text of this work was written in Chinese. The translator, editor, and publisher have made every effort to ensure that the English-language version is as accurate as possible and in keeping with the artistic intent of the author. Because this work reflects a different culture, some of the ideas and attitudes may be unfamiliar to the English-language audience.